PRAISE FOR FAR WARS

"After thousands of years of suffering and near annihilation, the human race is stronger and wiser, living in peace with other races. But the terror of the alien Kaarrk Swarm lurks beyond the dust clouds and dim light years of far space, threatening to destroy civilization and humankind." Well-written and stylish, the story opens in a distant future planet where two soldiers, one a student and the other a princess, fall in love only to be destined to fight an immutable army, one that might crush humanity throughout the universes. With skill and authority the author brings the story to a sharp climax. This is a short read and should appeal to fans of far future science fiction and space opera. Very vivid world-building!
—D. L. Cannon (Deborah Cannon, author of *The Pirate Empress* and many other acclaimed works).

"For fans of Cordwainer Smith, Jack Vance, and other far-future science fiction writers, FAR WARS will be a treat. Author John Argo creates and sustains an almost melancholy mood in this tale of love and adventure in far-off centuries to come, when a commoner falls in love with a daughter of the ruling body and is himself taken into that stratum of society. And then their home world is attacked by an implacable foe.... Suffice it to say that I read it in one sitting."
—A. L. Sirois (Pushcart Prize nominee and author of many works including *The Bohemian Magician*, *Detonator*, and other acclaimed works).

Far Wars

War and Peace 8000 Years From Now

A Far Future Science Fiction Novel in the

Empire of Time Series

by

John Argo

Clocktower Books, San Diego

Far Wars: War and Peace 8000 Years From Now

—This novel in several editions, and/or excerpts, was previously published in 2019 as *Star Clans of Corduwaine*, in 2016 as *Moon Berry Wine,* and in 2015 as *Tellerine*. The Corduwaine title is a reference to the late, great SF author Cordwainer Smith. Tellerine, the name of the world in which the story takes place, refers to the Turkish folk song as sung by Zara and by the late Ahmet Kaya.
—The characters and situations in this novel are fictional and do not represent any real-life persons, places, or situations. Any resemblance, although utterly unlikely, is purely coincidental.

—Clocktower Books, a San Diego small presss, and early Internet publisher, continues its pioneering tradition: "Exciting Books for Avid Readers on the Web Since 1996"
Clocktower Books
P. O. Box 600973
Grantville Station 92160
San Diego, California 92160-0973

E-Mail Contact: Editor/Publisher
editorial@clocktowerbooks.com
You can find us online at www.clocktowerbooks.com

Contents

DEDICATIONS

Cordwainer Smith

To my all-time favorite science fiction author Cordwainer Smith (Paul M. A. Linebarger, 1913-1966), whose short life was as remarkable and accomplished as his tiny oeuvre, but mighty and powerful literary gift to the world. My far future star system Corduwaine is named in his honor.

Telgrafin Tellerine

As well to the great Kurdish-Turkish singer and poet Ahmet Kaya (1957-2000) for his soulful rendition of Telgrafin Tellerine, the Turkish folk song that strongly influenced the tragic side of this novel, and gave its name to the planet-world Tellerine on which this epic centers.

I dedicate it just as much to talented Kurdish-Turkish singer Zara whose graceful and uplifting rendition of Telgrafin Tellerine drove the overall music of this novel from start to end.

For me, the powerful human drama of Far Wars represents a coming together of the Empire of Time themes of the human future, which I first explored as a passionate teenage novelist in Summer Planets (completed 1969 at age 19). I have since written many stories set in the Empire of Time universe. In Far Wars, Zara's Tellerine played in my head the whole time, while Ahmet's rendition took over during the fatal but heroic battle episode involving the heroic Princess Zara Upholder.

Many versions of the folk song can be found at YouTube and other venues, from cultures around the greater Aegean region. Ahmet's and Zara's are for me the most touching, gracefully paced, and spiritual.

My hope is that, in recognizing the universality of human experience, we can one day lay aside our differences and enjoy equality and happiness for every soul in this brief life and this vast universe.

So Many Others

From a lifetime of joyful reading, I have gratefully received much from many. Readers will find traces of diverse flavorings in this story from Isaac Asimov (Foundation) to Homer (Iliad, Odyssey), from Andre Norton (Star Traders) to Ray Bradbury (The Golden Apples of the Sun); I can only mention a few.

I have translated the poetry of Rainer Maria Rilke (Autumn Day) and Catullus (Sparrows), and loved the science fiction in Archibald

McLeish (Epistle To Be Left in the Earth) and T.S. Eliot (Four Quartets).

I sailed from Carthage on a penteconter with Aeneas, gazing toward the high, tragic fire of Dido forever lighting the night sky behind us. I grieved with Cicero over his Tullia and Martial over his Erotion, as well as my own Jennifer.

I soared across universes with Olaf Stapledon, and I cried in rain with Roy Batty in Blade Runner as he recounted his grand vision of stars fighting on the shoulder of Orion and an attack fleet burning like a match before forever disappearing.

So many stars to see, so little time to travel. We must make the most of our moment before the sea at night, with our feet upon sand like stars, and our eyes uplifted to stars like sand. We are stardust, as the song says, and it is indeed golden to inhale the sweet wind.

More Info at Rear

Much info about it all on my primary site:

www.johntcullen.com

See also rear of this book for info about the Empire of Time series, plus my DarkSF tales (motto: "DarkSF is the Dark Chocolate of Speculative Fiction").

Chapter 1. Tulearth

Everything that happened began with love. It was for love, for Zara, or even for humankind if I may permit myself such a lofty crown. She taught me so much. Sometimes I think she walks beside me wherever I go. She guides and teaches, but also laughs and loves in the shades of my dreams.

Soon after Zara and I met, I set aside my plans, and journeyed to the Corduwaine system to ask her father to bless the union we pledged together in the monastery gardens of Tulearth.

I was a young man tending a garden full of flowers under a powder-blue, perfect sky when I first saw her come in on the tiled, colorful walkways amid roses and jasmines. I had no idea who she was. I could see how beautiful were her long legs, her honey hair, her blue eyes, and well-proportioned features. The summer was as young as we were. I noticed several tall, slender young women on distant paths in the great gardens of Tulearth university. Like Zara, they strode in gracefully wind-blown sheer robes of subdued colors. They laughed and chattered happily—with just that cutting sharpness that the young can have when they joke about life and love, but especially about this boy or that girl. And what else would young women chatter about on such a perfect day?

I paused over my hoe and rested, watching them. I had my share of girls and drink, during my student days, so what could I make of these? They looked a few years younger, maybe new to the university, while I would soon to leave on my first astropath assignment. We lived an age of innocence, about to be ripped out of its sockets and thrown to hell by a massive, surprise Swarm invasion.

The beautiful young women's intrusion in those peaceful gardens was an excuse to rest and catch my breath. I grinned widely, panting, in the thick air that buzzed with bees and nuzzled with flower-seeking butterflies. I fancied myself to be as seductive as I was arrogant. In the summer heat, I wore only a gray, dingy loincloth and I must have been a sight. My sandal-shod feet were black with damp soil halfway up to my knees. My long, wavy dark hair dripped with sweat down to my shoulders, and my face was no doubt smeared with clay, through which my dark blue eyes must have looked startled and hungry. It is the instant language of young men and women, understood by two hearts. I wrote by hand in ink on a paper notebook an evening soon after, when my heart had become prisoner: "We flutter toward each other just as butterflies nuzzle dewy chalices of red and yellow and white flowers that wait for them in pregnant silence."

Zara Upholder separated from her ladies and became just an attractive young woman climbing through the clodded soils among flowers and vines as she drew near me. The fateful look had by that moment already passed between us across the distance. Zara caught my gaze as mine locked into hers—a fateful instant, when our lives were sealed forever. Something like a cloud of desire or shock passed over the meadow line of her forehead. While her two companions obliviously laughed and chattered, she almost floated toward me. Instantly and instinctively, more than anything else in the world, we longed to be with each other. She strode toward me over the black clods of soil I had turned in the last hour, as if she were gliding on the air with her new leather sandals and perfectly formed golden toes. Her face was both beautiful and handsome, and her sky-blue eyes barely registered any shyness. She was always sure of herself. She captured me into the nets of her beauty. I gave no resistance, but surrendered gladly.

"Do you have any moon berries, brother?" she asked in a strong, clear voice. She came to me in a flight of blown sugary silk and saffron-yellow shawls, all billowing in that early summer wind of Tulearth. Her caramel limbs moved in a scaly mermaid glow, faintly but seductively under those flowing garments. "What is your name?"

"Ranay Fennelon."

"Ranay is a handsome name. What does it mean?"

"It's a very ancient Earth name. It means Reborn."

"What an odd, quaint idea." She wrinkled her pippish nose, then sprinkled laughter. "I'm Zara Upholder from Tellerine." She thus offered me a door, open to make acquaintance, and I gladly entered her realm. I did nor realize just then that she was a kind of wealthy royalty, as passes for nobility among the freeholders of Tellerine. She was high-born and well bred, a crown princess of the Upholder clan, so into her realm I swam like a deep-cruiser fish with glowing scales.

"I think I have heard of it," I said diplomatically, embarrassed at my ignorance. I had no idea who the Upholders were, nor where or what

Tellerine was.

"Now about those moon berries," she said imperiously, positioning her fine legs apart to stride under that long sheer gown.

"Oh yes, come this way; I'll show you."

Her ladies in waiting stood on the colorfully tiled path, the one a study in billowing brown, the other in dark-red wine. They did not follow her, but maintained a respectful distance. Two or three young military priestesses in jet black joined them, with weapons visible in holsters; their faces looked pale as they glared in my direction. I started to realize that I was in august company. I was just young enough not to be much impressed, nor to care. After all, this beautiful young woman was no older than I was, and no doubt sat in the same seats and took the same techs and examinations as anyone else. That was the wonderful atmosphere at Holy Mother's University on Tulearth: Liberty, Equality, Sorority for all, regardless of personal accidents of birth or position.

"Your timing is good. The moon berries are in full bloom," I told her without using the formal address that would have subordinated me immediately. I was brash and sure of myself, just a shade shy of rude.

"Can you show them to me, Ranay?" She loved my freshness, and we both knew it. It was clearly what she wanted. "I wonder if the good brothers would object if my ladies carried off enough for a jar or two of fresh jam." She added with a twinkle in her eyes: "I would of course bribe you with a jar as well, so we are all in it together."

I set my hoe aside and waved for her to follow. "If heads must roll, let ours all roll together." The good brothers she referred to were the monks who tilled these gardens, just as they taught courses at the university. None of the mossy-green-robed friars dedicated to the Holy

Mother was anywhere to be seen at that moment. I was already on punishment duty, and might have incurred more if the wrong brother saw me. Of course I didn't care. What was another day of toiling in the garden in exchange for a few moments of such exquisite company?

We laughed, as we did much in months to come. She followed, and stumbled. I quickly reached out. She extended a strong, dry hand and took my dusty fingers with her firm grip. It was impressive to see how she balanced and steadied herself, a study in gracefulness with her long, full, athletic limbs and soft flanks. We walked, like two dancers in a minuet, holding our hands high together, as I guided her to the shady wall of bushes at the monastery wall. She foundered just a bit, when I was already on the walk way, so I turned and offered her both hands. She almost fell into my arms, but quickly recovered with a somewhat sheepish look while her ladies looked on with blank expressions.

The shady side of the chapel wall was thickly carpeted with hollygloss, whose leafy shade was filled with juicy, pale mirabels or moon berries.

"You are not an ordinary monk, are you?" she said in a low, conspiratorial tone so only she and I could hear. Now we stood facing each other on the walkway at the edge of the labyrinth of flowers and trimmed hedges, pent in by high gray ways drowning in ivy and sunshine. Beyond the walls loomed the blue-black slate tiles of the university, and the attendant town and temples.

"Not at all," I told her. "I'm a third year cadet, doing penance for a night on the town when I should have been grinding for my astrotex."

"I thought so," she said with visible relief. The unspoken message was that she'd be mortified had she realized she'd been flirting with a young man of the noviate who would never taste nectar like hers.

The love story is one I have written down and filed among the screens and cables of Upholder libraries on Tellerine. We need not dwell much more on it here. Zara and I became inseparable. We would go running together on wet sand at the ocean's edge while dawn fog drifted over the thundering breakers, while heavy-breasted white sea birds screeched over the black, wet cliffs where they mated, and where they guarded their nests.

Zara was a tall, strong young woman with tight muscles and soft skin. We became lovers and pledged our lives to each other. "I love you more than I love my life itself," she told me on two occasions with that earnest look. Her eyes were blue as moon berries, white as milk, in skin the color of honey with just a berry flush on the cheek bones. She let me gather her thick, wild auburn hair in my hands, and readily let me pull her toward me among the sheets of her bed or mine in the turreted dorms of Tulearth university.

She was competitive, by her nature. Often our morning or evening beach runs became a race. The Upholder have a gesture for combat or competition. They raise their hands, palms facing forward, with the elbows close together and the hands parallel as if doing a pull-up; and they close their fists. It is the strapping-in of a pilot going to war in space. It is the athlete lowering herself into a steel sled for a competitive mountain run in snow and mist while the Tellerine sun glows like a tangerine ball among cotton clouds. It is a universally understandable "Let's go!" and "Follow me!" or a boisterous "Today we win or die!"

And of course she had the chopped laugh of her clan, the crazy war cry. "Come and get me if you can!" And off we went at whatever sport we decided to play there on Tulearth or later on Tellerine. We'd let each other win sometimes, or we'd go all out and beat each other to the goal. I think we were about fifty fifty for real wins, if you cut out the laughing, the jostling, the fake fighting, the play wrestling, and sometimes the stopping to grapple, throw clothes over our shoulders, and wetly and noisily screw on the damp, cold sand under gray dawn clouds. Even at that she was competitive, pounding away hip to hip from above or below, so that I felt like a boat in a storm at sea (and loved it to ecstasy).

We completed university about the same time, and grew totally in love with each other. I sent videx home to my family on Luxanne world, saying I would would not let them down, but I must take time from my plans to explore something very important. My family responded with some disappointment but with encouragement and solidarity nonetheless. For privacy reasons, out of sheer discretion, I did not mention that I was traveling to Tellerine in the Corduwaine system to propose marriage to an Upholder woman. The very idea would have frightened my mother.

We were ordinary people, though we were exemplary citizens in our small town on Luxanne, System Mirmar, in the Sea of Colored Glass, on the Rifraf Arm of the galaxy.

The long Inversion was over, humankind was free once again by treaties and commercial bonds, to travel and trade among our former enemies and oppressors.

We were no longer a hunted species, but back in the mainstream of interstellar breeds.

Life was still normal then, before the Kaarrk Swarm attacks. We thought our long night was over. Eternal vigilance is the price of liberty. Ignore history, relearn it all over again the hard way.

Chapter 2. Tellerine

Zara and I arrived at Tellerine by separate Temporale ships (for propriety and protocol), coincidentally while a ceremonial convoy with a large military train was just bringing Holy Mother the Popess to Tellerine on her first state visit since the beginning of ManTime, the end of the Inversion. We had no idea, of course—nobody did—that humansh and alienoid traitors watched and reported every move back via subether to a secret Kaarrk Swarm advance base on the fringes of the Corduwaine system.

Fifteen ships of the line floated out of the Temporale, the transit world outside time and space, wormhole network of key points in our visible universe. Among the vessels was the gold and white cruiser carrying the spiritual leader and ruler of humankind.

Zara and I were eager to be together again after our separation. Protocol allowed us to sit together in a chartered airliner that brought us from the orbital station to the great Upholder starfield in Corduwaine. We sat in adjacent chairs, holding hands, and looking out the porthole over a quadrille sprawl of city lights. Zara with her free hand showed me points of interest. She was excited to be home again, now a Master of Starflight Science, as I was also since we had both graduated from

Tulearth. She had left her family as a growing girl, and now returned as an educated woman and a leader to be.

She pointed to the ruined, truncated pyramid of the Mercury Fortress looming far away. She told me the name of a golden bay I saw shining in evening sunlight, where she had loved surf sailing under Upholder colors, which are dark wine-red. That was the Bay of Lue by the Sea of Blue. Whether it was sports, commerce, or just plain governing, her blood was about competition and winning. The way she squeezed my hand, it was clear that I was one of her victories. "You looked like such a wild man," she confided in me once as we nuzzled in bed, while rain pattered and splattered from Tulearth turrets and slate-lined domes. "You wore just a dirty loincloth, and I kept hoping it would fall down. I wanted to rip it off you with my teeth and lick you." We both laughed, that night in her dorm. "Your hair stuck straight out in all directions, and you have these beautiful evening-blue eyes. I loved how white and even your teeth were when you grinned at me. I wanted to take your grin home in a jar to treasure it."

"Well, here I am," I told her. "Grin and all." I rested half-upright beside her as she nuzzled in the crook of my arm. I ran a hungry hand down the long, firm slopes of her body. When I had her rear in my hand, she sighed sexually and pressed closer to me. She reached down and took me in her hand. She held my fullness with both hands, gently as if it were a butterfly, and guided it to her waiting chalice. A thousand times I took her to me, and she gave herself, taking me in arms so strong they seemed desperate—and the harsh desire in her breath affirmed what she told me: "I love you more than my life itself."

We came to Tellerine, where she was fourth or fifth in line to become the next Trask. She had two older brothers, military pilots and commercial doctors both, named Romen and Caleo. They were handsome, of course, in that athletic, horse-riding manner of the Tellerine nobility. Their wives—my new sisters to be—were a bit like Zara in spirit as well as in that sportsy, healthy, plain but attractive way. The women, though not directly related except through marriage, all seemed to have that same bony, athletic, horsy, handsome easy-riding confidence of power and wealth. Zara's two sisters were dark Caliste and young, pretty Artemi.

Caliste was married to a young man of the Sender clan on the other side of the world. Caliste was wiry and dark-skinned, with a frizz of black hair, and eyes as fiery as they were olive colored. Only the facial features and the athletic limbs gave way their parallel lineage. Trask had been a busy man in his youth, siring offspring with half a dozen prominent daughters of other clans, in the accepted custom of their world.

Trask, in his old age, was still a robust figure with wild snowy hair and challenging gray eyes. He was my height (medium), with a steely paunch. He wore plain gray wool and brown leathers, including a wide belt and matching boots of farmed fawn leather. He welcomed me into his innermost study. It was a place few men or women ever saw, so I felt privileged. Zara, choosing a young wild man in a garden many parsecs away, had willed it. Otherwise, I would have never set foot in this rarified atmosphere.

The hardness around his mouth told implicitly how he became one of the world's richest freeholders. We met soon after my arrival—why waste time?—in a library study high in the family fortress overlooking the city of Zond with its flags and lakes and many lights on day and night, or were they myriad windows glowing golden in Corduwaine sunlight? Trask walked with a slight limp, and held himself a bit sideways, from old sporting or war injuries. He didn't offer, and I didn't ask. Frankly, my mouth was dry and I felt intimidated as two eunuchine droidals ushered us across a sea of carpets, past astrolabes and other affectations, among wall maps of seas of stars, to a pillared window where the famous general awaited me. Zara was his favorite child, and Trask wanted to examine me under a microscope. Apparently, he already knew everything about me, and liked what he saw. His voice had a mix of abrasiveness and affection in its timbre as he pumped my hand. "Welcome, my boy. How was your trip?"

"Uneventful, my lord. It's the best one can ask."

"Well said, lad. Come, let me offer you a robust little shalignac to warm your synapses." He led me to a darkly gleaming table covered in leather, with a plate of sea-green glass over it. There, he poured us each a finger-glass of amber liquor. We toasted, clinking our glasses gently together. He asked me about my family as we sipped the sweet, fiery moon berry liquor. "My daughter seems to be in your spell."

"I am more in her spell, lord."

He laughed a bark. "Hah! Her mother still has me enchanted, the witch. Poor thing, she died a few years ago. We all miss her so much. Yet I am a happy fool these days. Run while you can, my boy. Run for your life. Once you are in their grip, there is no escape."

I held the little glass to my shoulder and looked out over the misty seas and streets. "I have lost all desire for freedom."

"You've got it bad," he barked. "We'll have to give you care and attention. I understand you have rank."

"I am an officer, sir."

"A cub."

"Admittedly."

"Left junior, I imagine?"

"Yessir. Soon to be senior tenant." Those are military ranks. Ironically, their family name (Upholder) in part derives from the vassalage. Tenant and holder are from the same root of meaning. I could have looked it up in the electropedias of his faux libraries in that room. I am a lover of etymologies—the archeology and paleontology of words and their meanings. Trask was a generalissimo of land forces as well as a supreme admiral of his system's fleets. Both of his older sons—Zara's brothers—were wing commander pilots in the star fleet of that particular ocean of stars, known as the Sea of Green Glass in the ancient Mercurian system of stellar mapping, thousands of years ago when there was a mythological Earth Home, lost during the two thousand year Inversion.

"Excellent," rasped my father-to-be. "You won't find any special treatment among us." He dug a rough elbow into my side. "Nor will we oppose your rise in rank and influence." He gave me a conspiratorial laugh and a wink with wild eyebrows. It meant he had accepted me into the clan's power structure. I was free to stay, to marry his daughter, to become his son, and to be his vassal. I was scared to death, as much as I was head over heels in love with Zara. All my plans, my future, my hopes and dreams, were now phantoms as the new reality set in. I had not yet decided that I would spend the rest of my life here on this world that seemed like the inside of a shalignac bottle: heady, rich, swirling with potential and destiny, yet a stale end of contentment. To a young man, it was the death of adventure, the little death of orgasm, the harness of adulthood when I was still a stallion galloping break-neck I knew not where nor did I care.

"We will take good care of you," Trask said. "You will take care of Zara, and she knows how to take care of herself. You couldn't ask for a stronger or better woman to be your wife."

"I humbly admit to my great fortune, lord." My knees were knocking together, and my teeth chattering at the enormity of the pact I was making with this violent goat who could have me disappear if I showed any sign of violating his powerful trust. He was a war lord, beneath the civil veneer. All people of such power and station are war lords who will stop at nothing to hold their fiefdoms together.

Before the official announcements, followed by my formal request for Zara's hand, and Trask's welcoming me into his family, I would live separately in the city. The clan had large office buildings with internal apartments. By that I mean quiet, echoing halls with central gardens and fountains, surrounded by luxurious suites full of filtered sunlight from alabaster and soapstone skylights. All manner of quiet servants moved quietly about cleaning, serving, and obeying. I could have had all sorts of interesting women for company, but I am a man of principle. I chose to have Zara and her sisters visiting me at every opportunity. Sometimes they brought their husbands as well, all but sweet young Artemi who regarded me with intoxicated eyes.

Trask kept me busy and put me to work in the city. I was to become the ammanus or right hand man of a talented older executive named Charlemain. Charlemain de Granger was from lesser nobility in the northern lakes region of Tellerine's largest continent. He was a chubby man with a hard face, gone totally gray, with colorless eyes and personality, but hard and capable the way Trask liked his executives to be. Trask was a generalissimo, and these were his colonels. As it turned out, I barely met Granger before the war, so there's not much to tell about—he and his family were all killed in the first days of massive bombing.

My family were to come from Luxanne and stay with us for the ceremony. That meant my father Vilo, an agricultural domineer on our home world of Luxanne, my mother who taught mathematics at the Uni, my brother Manel, and my sisters Livin and Haril. That was the plan, until the Swarm attacked.

It seems the Holy Mother and her entourage, as well as two high-ranking flag officers of the Arm governance, had deorbited and were now guests of the Tellerine Administration in Mayeril.

In retrospect, those weeks of innocence and joy were the happiest of my life. I was about to marry into the wealthiest of the powerful clans of Tellerine. I remember long, wonderful afternoons under the lingering sun on the great lawns of Upholder House in the northern suburbs of Corduwaine. The captains and their wives of the military came and went at endless champagne parties, because Romen and Caleo were both handsome army officers and these were their colleagues at polo, at maneuvers, at political jostling around the council and parliament. Caliste Sender, a dusky, slender Upholder beauty with a ball of black frizzy hair and evening-blue eyes presided over cocktail parties, always with lingering looks toward me. Her husband, a powerful but bullish-looking older man, had been a political choice of Trask. I think, in all honesty, that Caliste was a tragic figure; her eyes betrayed longing and hunger; I could almost hear her long, silent cry for rescue. Zara must have known, but she didn't renounce her sister. There was, rumor had it, another sister somewhere floating out there, a twin of Zara's but Zara avoided the subject. Zara was, if anything, loyal to a fault. She was an Upholder before anything else. She was Trask's absolute favorite, and he treated her like a crown princess—which she was, in effect, though the Tellerine people avoided all pretenses at monarchy and empire. Tellerine culture was austere and business-oriented, although obviously they had the same oligarchs and aristocrats as any other society. By contrast, my home world of Luxanne was too simple and under populated—an agricultural backwater—to have anything more than wealthy, drunken ranchers and bloated country club doctors and lawyers for an upper crust.

Caliste clearly would have run away if it were not for family loyalty. I think it is the reason Zara nurtured and supported her, to keep her in the fold, maybe even to prevent scandal if Caliste ran away. Caliste contented herself with displays of wealth, while her husband was usually away on business, much of it offworld and outsystem. I can't imagine how lonely and frustrated she was.

One delight was the youngest sister, Artemi. She was at that awkward phase between being a girl and a woman. Artemi was a tall, willowy girl like Zara, with crystal blue eyes and long, straight hair the color of a sunset, when the last golden yellow is driven out by a growing forest-brown duskiness. Women on Tellerine grow their hair long. It is beaten and blanched and discolored by the sun like old clothes faded in streaks and patches, and yet that makes it all the more beautiful. Zara says it gives them character. I came to understand that, like many other strange and musky and potent things about their culture.

Artemi was somehow encrushed (as they say) with the intoxicating anticipation of Zara's upcoming marriage with me. Like a flash of light in an afternoon window, Artemi attached herself to us. I could swear she was pretending to be Zara, and playing at being wedded. Often she came and held my hand as if we were engaged. She loved to sit with me when three or four of us went to the Blue Sea, to the Bay of Lue, to threevees in the city, to musical shows, or just to eat iced meloncolion on the showy balconies of the corniche. Zara would spend much leisurely time combing Artemi's long hair with a tortoise shell comb while the girl made teenage eyes at me.

We would tease her (not too cruelly): "So, Artemi, when are you getting married? Are you engaged yet? Is there a Sender at your door?" She would wrinkle her lip up in disgust at the name of Caliste's husband. "Is there a Charger or a Disdainer or a Victor calling on you? Some handsome young man with sunny eyes and a surfy smile?"

"Stop it!" she blurted once, with tears springing to her eyes, and Zara and I hugged her before she ran off to die in an emotional thunderstorm someplace, only to be reborn an hour later, running in the surf barefoot with two or three other beautiful wealthy young girls.

Zara whispered to me that night: "Artemi is planning to be my bridesmaid. That is what all the serious study and obsession with detail is all about. That's the meaning behind all the little rituals like serving tea and cake, or braiding my unbraidable hair, or looking through a thousand videx catalogs of wedding ensembles."

"My two young sisters are a lot like that," I said as Zara and I lay together, nude, with the Blue Sea breeze wafting across our patio and through the double doors into our hideaway on the estate.

Zara added with a sad little smile: "I think Caliste wishes you would marry her."

"I would," I teased, "but Tellerine is monogamous."

Zara shoved me gently. "You could not handle more than one Tellerine woman."

"I can't handle even one." I buried my mouth in her neck and blew, making a farting noise on her skin.

She rolled over, pulled me down on her with both firm hands on the small of my back, and cupped my naked rear cheeks. It was dark, and I could only make out her long, pale slender form. Moonlight faintly illumined the wet glints of her eyes and lips. "Do that again," she said in a low, dangerous voice: "Down here." I felt her knees move apart.

Chapter 3. Attack

The world as we had known it ended not long after that. On a fateful day, I was walking through the busy streets of Trzond, a suburb of Corduwaine, with Zara on my mind. We were to have lunch at a restaurant with lake views, smothered in trees, on a resort island in the bay. As I stood waiting for the ferry, it seemed as if the sky darkened slightly.

All of us strangers froze and looked upward amid a rushing, thundering sound. As inexplicable explosions echoed around the sky, it sounded like furniture being dragged across a wooden floor—but deafening, and instantly punctuated by explosions and red flashes. Smells of fire, burning tar, whatever, violently permeated the air. Smoke drifted recklessly, disregarding normalcy and customary order.

The surprise attack on the Corduwaine system had begun. Kaarrk Swarm legions emerging from deep Temporale transit space smashed through light years of humansh systems, seeking to kill the heart of us, to kill us all and our alienoid allies, or enslave us in yet another Inversion of Humankind lasting centuries or maybe forever.

Unsuspecting citizens all around me looked up with startled, innocent, curious faces. Soon, our expressions turned to alarm, then terror.

Legions of Kaarrk Swarm fighter craft streaked through the clouds over head. Guided by infrasight, they could shoot through cloud cover, by day or night. The Kaarrk swarmed like flies. Each time a new squadron exploded into the atmosphere from space, their limitless numbers spattered like fast-moving grain shot.

As buildings began to topple around me, and the screams of the trapped and dying floated pitifully in the smoky air, I raised my hand to summon my personal holog. Instantly a small image of the Trask lobby appeared in the air just off-center by my right temple. The young men and women staff could be seen bravely staying at their consoles to work the emergency com, even as the building shook around them and lumina fell and shattered on spacious lobby floors.

Running for the nearest pubtrans, I hollered "Override, override, override!" Even with my high Upholder priority I could not get a dedicated spectrum. All hell had broken loose.

The pubtrans tubes were collapsed. I came to a descending stairwell (Trzond) choked with rubble and colorful blotches I took to be women's and children's summer dresses, immobile and gory in the stones.

Kaarrk Swarm attack aerons kept streaking by, and the explosions continued, as did screams on the streets. Howling sirens added to the madness as they kept up an unbroken wail of agony over a suddenly broken world. Tracers rose in to the air. Artillery *boom, boom, boom*ed and the ground shook. Kaarrk arrow-fliers ripped the sound barrier with an unfolding boom that rattled *tat-tat-tat-tat* as they echoed away over the horizon, only to be drowned out by the next peristalsis of death puke, wave of nausea, tidal comb of terror.

I reached the Upholder precinct at Trask 501 and entered the lobby, after showing my palm holo i.d. to several armed and hysterical elder guards. Trask himself was at a distant resort with his current wife and children, but he was live now on holog. "Take command of the city," he barked at me. "The admin building has been hit—of course—the Swarm took out all the infrastructure. I am declaring you Master of Circumstance." I assumed that meant something important on Tellerine. It did.

"What about Zara?"

"She is assisting her brothers on the flight line."

I spoke the commands to switch holog from Trask to Zara on our private com line.

"My love," she said in the small threevee holog before my pained eyes.

"Come be with me," I said. If I asked anything of fate, I would give anything, but that I wanted more than anything in the world.

"I love you more than my life itself," she said. The truth of her words radiated in her eyes. Behind her stood her brothers wearing flight suits getting ready to board orbital fighter craft. "My heart is in your heart," she promised. "My soul is in your hands. My poor body only has to be here with the fighters. You will be with me every moment."

I couldn't speak, only nod. I loved her more than I loved my own life. So she got busy with the work she must do in support of the air fighters and orbital scramblers. Our first line of defense had been broken, and they were bravely putting it together again one dead pilot at a time.

I busied myself with the defense of the city. One by one, surviving ward captains crawled out of the rubble and presented themselves at my headquarters, either via holog or in the person of the bloodied, dusty survivor himself, herself.

We learned that the Bay of Lue, on whose shore the Holy Mother and the generals were camped in glory, had been reduced to molten glass and glowing slag. The Kaarrk knew exactly where to strike. Hot winds swirled on that new plain, where today the 300 brave ones march arm-in-arm with their glowing boots. The legend carved on the base of the Lue obelisk reads: *Non Quam Post Hac*, or simply NQPH in ancient alphabetics, Never Again.

At one point, our artillery brought down a low-flying Kaarrk fighter craft. I was called away from my duties directing a growing army of survivors and rescue workers to see if we could take prisoners. With me were several military priestesses including an abbess from the diocese of Corduwaine, plus a troop of civil defense fighters, and various other dusty looking souls. We came to the smoking hole where a hotel for star travelers had been, not far from the space port. Deep in the hole was a reddish glow. Acrid smoke rose in a foul greenish-khaki cloud whose color and stench remain burned into my memory. Along with an armed priestess and a scientist, I ordered the others to stay above and form a safety cordon. Then we three clambered down over the hot rubble toward a chamber carved from hell itself. We found there a shattered metal ship structure that had embedded itself in the smoldering ruins of underground halls and kitchens. Approaching slowly, our lips curled in disgust. We found the pilots of the murderous attack ship. It was the first and only time I would ever see the actual

Kaarrk who existed only to hate our kind, to kill us where they could. I think their only reason for existence was to be our enemies. What I saw looked like two bath tubs filled with huge glistening black shapes (eels, worms, scorpions) squirming in disarray amid their destroyed cockpit. It was probably only a pilot and co-pilot, but it looked like two snake pits. I saw at least six vaguely human-like faces on the many waving eel-suckers, looking at us open-mouthed with a mixture of rage, pain, and hatred. Their only real emotion in dying is a rage that they will not be able to hate any longer.

To my one side, the scientist said: "Should we call for a medical team? We can study them and learn—."

To my right side, the military priestess said: "We could get a platoon of medics in here and see what we can salvage—."

In my own emotional state, I took the flame thrower from the priestess and emptied its naphtha froth into the roiling snake pit of hatred and insanity. I belched the flames of hell down on them, watching them scream and melt in their final contortions, while the air filled with a stench somewhat like a mixture of burning sofas and barbecued space crabs in a gasoline sauce.

Nobody stopped me, and when the flame thrower was empty, I hurled it with both arms as far as I could into the black, dead hole where nothing survived. Without saying a word, the three of us turned and slowly walked out of the death mine. Hot wind swirled around us, blowing embers and cinders and black flakes like snow in hell.

If I could have spoken, I might have said: "Bring me all the devils in hell and I will do the same to every last one of them." But I was speechless.

We all understood the history behind this. Humankind had emerged from its evolutionary home, a planet now lost to an unknown fate, and had conquered much of the galaxy. As is the manner of our race, we brought with us the highest good intentions, in the form of the Holy Mother and her Church, but also the usual evils of greed and power madness. After centuries of misrule, our alien subjects attacked the City of the Universe, Mercury Free Port City, and destroyed our empire. Humans became the hunted, the hated, the hopeless. Where the alien races did not exterminate us on sight, or hunt us like vermin, they enslaved us. Nothing could be more cruel than some of the damage we did to ourselves, especially the human brain boxes and other genetic crimes. We were our own worst enemies, and paid for two thousand years in the Inversion of Man. Now we live in the Renaissance, in ManTime. So the Kaarrk Wars were a throwback to those evil and painful centuries. Just when we thought we had peace and freedom, along came these monsters who would turn every habitable planet into a roiling snake pit for their soulless, mindless tangle of shuddering disgust. You see from my language that it isn't possible for me to maintain the kind of even, objective attitude like that of the Holy Mother when She speaks from the throne of love for all life. I notice that the holy and blessed military priestess made no effort to yank the flame belcher from my enraged grip as I torched those death-pukers to a crisp.

We are all human, which is what gives us our flawed humanishness. Amen, I say. Homen, as they say across the galactic seas wherever humans build fires and warm themselves, telling stories while they eat bread and drink wine. Our weapons are ever handy. We have learned. Never again.

Chapter 4. Corduwaine

A holog from Zara came to me on the second day of war, when she stood before my eyes—or her shimmering image in a darkened flight bay—in an olive-drab flight suit, holding a black glowing bubble helmet under one articulated arm. Her beautiful wild honey hair lifted in an oily hangar breeze.

I had just been given a window office on a twentieth story tower, formerly a hotel owned by Trask of course, now a civil defense emergency headquarters. The windows were gone, shattered, and smoky air drifted by. Fires still burned and smoked across the city. Those who had been injured were dead or silent. The only sounds that came up were the occasional belch of ak-ak fire, puffs of black smoke in the sky, and the screaming of some fighter craft—whether our own, or a probing Kaarrk scout plane we had no idea. The CD people fired at anything that moved, even our own stuff, so jittery was everyone. I finally had to order a cease fire just so our own people would not injure each other.

The first damage reports were horrific. The Holy Mother and the general staff had all perished. The death toll climbed into many digits. All defense communications nerve centers on the planet had been punched out. The Kaarrk surprise attack had been extremely thorough and successful. We tried calling the perimeter stations in space, but everything was dead. Tellerine has three small moons—all three were knocked out of com net. The satellites and solar stations had all been wiped out. Worst of all, our surviving field detection grids revealed the ghostly outlines of at least four separate Kaarrk invasion fleets.

Everywhere in space for parsecs around were dogfights, in which our defenders died one by courageous one. We were outmanned, outgunned, and out-planned. Our situation grew more desperate, even hopeless, by the hour.

Yesterday, when I last spoke with Zara, that flight bay was filled with ships and pilots. Today it looked almost empty. Only off to one side were a half dozen reconnaissance fliers of an antiquated type. I knew from the many sources of criss-cross radio traffic intersecting at my GHQ that the mechanics had begun patching up old, abandoned scout fliers, outfitting them with primitive bombs and outdated lightgray shooters. Anything that would fly into orbit or beyond was being patched together in our desperate effort to avert annihilation, or at least hold the Kaarrk Swarm back long enough for a rescue fleet to arrive from far Karayol or Tulearth in a matter of days via the Temporale—if the Kaarrk were not destroying that ancient netpath itself, which vectored space and time lines.

Our situation was more desperate than even I realized. The Kaarrk had cut off our lines of communication with rear commands. The Corduwaine system was a strategic hub in the Temporale transit network. Hour by hour, it became clear that the Kaarrk were already attacking light years beyond the ruins of the Corduwaine system. Their objective was to neutralize the main star wall perimeter of the humansh command system in the Sea of Sapphire Stars, where a good half of surviving humankind occupied a thousand or more habitable worlds. If they could punch through and raid those planets, they would destroy half of humankind in a short time. Then they could organize a *jihate* against the remainder of our race, and purge us from existence in service of their incomprehensible madness.

Since they do not have individual life, they cannot comprehend us. They live as worms, and die as worms. The individual has no meaning. They have only meaning in the unitary central emo of their race, said to be a huge blob of gelly residing in a honeycomb slime nest orbiting a dim green star in the Sea of Fear (name given by the one humansh explorer craft that entered their system and emerged to tell about it).

"My love."

"Zara."

"I am going out on patrol."

"No. I need you with me. I need you to be safe."

"My brothers are both dead. There is an empty commander's seat on a fighter craft."

"But you are not a trained fighter."

"My brothers spent many hours teaching me. There is nobody else left to fly, to lead the eleven pilots waiting for a main chop."

"Zara."

"I love you more than I love my own life."

I blew her a kiss. There wasn't time for anything else. My office had four doors, all of them now rattling with urgent pounding. Messages flowed in from the city, the government, the remaining space command. As the holog faded, and her beautiful face with it, I was torn across a hundred tasks.

The saying goes: "Send in the army and the police. When all else fails, send in the air marines. When even that fails, and everything is dead and lost, send in the military priestesses. They have such fighting rage or *macchia* that they will rip the dead out of their graves, and kill them again."

In those gloomy hours, I began to think we were beyond even that. We could fight, those of us who were left. We could slow the Kaarrk down. We could not stop them with out small, outgunned forces. Even our main systems far back were under serious assault, so they had no time or strategy for us. We had been given up as lost. Nobody had to tell me that. I knew it. Nobody had seen the Kaarrk coming. Now we had only a fight to our deaths left. All that in a matter of a few days. I did not have time to ponder the enormity or the suddenness.

We had emergency stations but no fully functioning field hospital. A group of monks from a local university were going to donate their lone standing structure—the chapel—along with their medical students to start a triage hospital. A hotel had underground parking that they proposed to offer as a makeshift recovery ward. A unit of military priestesses had flown in from Moon 3 to take charge of security; they were combat medical technicians, like all of their kind, besides being sacral death fighters; and would be assigned to staff the hotel ward. And so on. Bit by aching, painful bit, we were putting our lives back together while awaiting the next devastating punch from the Kaarrk Swarm.

I had to step back from it and speak with Trask, who arrived in a row of dark green armored flyers along with squads of air marines and military priestesses, all armed to the teeth and talking on hologs with unseen supervisors. Trask entered my GHQ and closed the door. He collapsed in a seat and started crying when we were alone together. His two sons had been killed, and his elder daughter was on her way into space. The husband of his daughter Caliste (the dark, frizzy-haired beauty) had been lost to a Kaarrk patrol over the orbiting moon reefs or lunaroids of Gandeleon, the fourth planet.

Trask Upholder recovered from his grief and said: "There is always something to salvage so we fight on."

"Yes, lord."

"You're holding the fort well, sonny."

"Thank you, sir." Dust floated by as we spoke. There were still occasional explosions. The air smelled of burning; I dared not imagine what. It was a stench you wanted to take pliers and tear out of your nostrils, but it gets imprinted in memory like a horrible nightmare and will never come out. I could not think that far ahead then, but I think back clearly to those hours, those days, every living today.

"I am going to convene the national government at Corduwaine North," Upholder told me as he extended wiry arm covered with gray hairs, and a red hand like the claw of a steel lobster. "Keep up the good work, Ranay. You are now the only son I have left."

"Then you approve of my marriage with Zara." I tried levity, but it sounded flat.

"I do." He pointed a scarred finger in my face. "You have no idea how many of the richest young men on this world have tried to ask for her, and were warned to avoid coming near me. You are the one and only, son." Suddenly overcome, he embraced me with that steely body and those powerful arms. No, he was not secretly a droid or a bot. He was an Upholder. That would scare even a fighting mech into running away.

"We will hold the city together," I promised him as he walked to the door.

He paused, while opening the door to reveal the waiting military priestesses outside. "I like that you say we. If you had said I, I would throw you out that window over there."

Trask, Lord Upholder, was that kind of guy. Nobody was tougher, not even among street thugs. Trask's steely knuckles had gotten everyone's attention. And yet he was respected enough offplanet and outsystem that the Holy Mother herself, along with important generals (the kind who only wear a lot of ribbons, and never actually any fighting) came to celebrate some Upholder family anniversary. They'd been in the Nostra Causa for many centuries and on many worlds. Truth was that there were Upholder septs and clans scattered throughout the Humansh Sea. If they lost their shirts here, the survivors could easily find refuge across far parsecs with blood relatives, and rebuild. But there lay the thing. What made the Upholder who they were. They were at their best when cornered, and loved digging in for a fight to the death. It was their most famous, terrifying, and lovely quality. In case you had not noticed, humankind did not bounce back from a 2,000 year Inversion with kid gloves. We had learned respect and humility. We had become more humane, not to make a pun. We humans are a pack of mythic wolverines, following leaders like Trask when need be. His kind always arise when history needs them. And then we can't get rid of them, but that's a matter for a peaceful, sunny day if we ever see another like it.

Chapter 5. Defenders

As commander of GHQ Corduwaine, I received all sorts of traffic, much of it privileged. By now I had a staff set up, so I had adjutants poring over the message traffic and prioritizing what came to my eyes and ears. I had dictated priorities to care for civilians, to shore up defensive positions, to organize whatever weapons and ammo we had left to fight with, and to get our holog net back up and running with high crypto override security characteristics. I had a whole field station of cryptog officers working on that stuff deep in the guts of Trask 501, so I could divert my attention to more humansh concerns.

At some point, a female orderly approached holding a transfer (portable holog platform). "Lord," she said, for now I was Trask Junior, so to speak, "you wanted to know about the 569th Civil Defense Squadron."

My head must have snapped up. "Yes?" I nearly broke my neck responding. "What?"

The orderly was a middle-aged female reservist in civilian clothing, wearing only her corps insignia and warrant officer tabs on the shoulders of a pink blouse hastily grabbed from a closet at the last moment, such a rabble were we. She said in a kindly voice, knowing the context: "You were interested in Zara Upholder's status."

I grabbed the platform from her hand and set it on the desk. Around me was a swirl of activity as men and women came and went. Construction crews arrived and built a temporary brick wall to replace the blown-out picture windows. They inset smaller storm windows until something more stylish could one day be built back in, if that day ever came. The smells of smoke and fire were almost gone, as were the smells of what was burning (including bodies). Civilization was returning, after a fashion.

On the desk, the orderly expanded the holog so its field occupied a cubic meter. "You were interested in this," she said. The image field spoke for itself. Earlier recorded images showed a squadron of Civil Defense scouts being readied in the hangar. One of the craft was shown frontally, so that I looked up toward the tiny cockpit slits. I could just barely make out that there were two pilots in the craft. I have no idea if Zara was one. I later learned they were all women reservists, with one military priestess who knew how to handle a spacer, and Zara as the wing leader. All you could see was the upper halves of two scrappy helmets, and the blackish sun visors that gave the wearer anonymity. I waved for the orderly to speed through the still shots to the live action. First I thought the screen was dead—then I realized we were seeing wingcam videx from a drone flying with the 569th CD Squadron.

Chapter 6. Behemoth

Tail markings on the delta wings clearly showed the 569th Civil Defense Squadron, and various Tellerine and Corduwaine insignia. The obsolete craft behaved nicely, skimming through the outer atmosphere of Moon 3. Seen at an opportune angle, their scissor wingtips left faint, parallel contrails on the air mass of this large satellite world.

The videx image switched back to the hangar on Tellerine. An older man in a colonel's uniform, spokesman for the air and space defense command, spoke to a historian's recorder. "The 569th are safely out of harm's way, patrolling a sector that has had no tactical activity during this entire conflict so far. In fact, because of a major disturbance several tellorbits further out from the sun, humansh forces have pulled all tactical units from this sector. I will bring you more news of that as it occurs. For now, our 569th scouts are scheduled to return to home base on Tellerine by local time 0700 which is roughly daybreak in Corduwaine, the planet's capital city. Switching back to our space videx..."

He chattered on. I did not want to embarrass Zara by cutting through with a direct line, as I could have as a primary ground commander. I had the legal and strategic right to cut in, but there were so many things wrong with that idea that I would not begin to count them. Begin with nepotism, favoritism, and so forth. To my eternal regret, I took the road of protocol and maintained a dignified, loving silence.

The demands of running a bleeding, gutted city full of wounded and dying people had my full attention once again. An hour went by, then another, and I was growing tired just staying on top of it. The orderly brought us lunch, and the staff and I forced ourselves to have a quarter hour behind locked doors as we chewed and sipped too tensely to enjoy whatever it was in those disposable containers. I remember they smelled faintly of salt and meat and sweet-sour sauces. We washed it down with citrus water frosted with mountain ice. Then it was back to work.

A commotion got our attention. Staff were gathering around the holog, which still showed that dull, unchanging shot of space—mainly night shots, with the delta winged CD fighters skimming over the atmosphere of Moon 3 leaving needle-sharp parallel contrails. It was as hypnotic as it was boring. But something was happening elsewhere in the Corduwaine solar system. Something big.

That aging colonel's voice was back as the holog showed a variety of still shots. Some were panoramic, others tight to very tight. I saw the Corduwaine sun, filtered of course; hard planets in silvery light with craters, and gas giants with colorful cyclones and bands. A major telescope was in play, fielded by a Moon 2-based astro defense technical unit. Normally, these are the folks who remain vigilant looking for incoming impactors like comets, meteors, or other debris.

The Kaarrk would have knocked them out, but somehow missed them, so our people deployed them.

The colonel's voice overrode: "The wave field wide sensors have determined a gravitational anomaly coming from outer space into the solar system. We can't see whatever it is, but we can detect its energy waves, kind of like the bow waves of a ship, both pushing and leaving a trail behind. Experts at Defense are telling me this is really, really big whatever it is. If you'll look closely you'll see what looks like fireflies in that general direction. Those are actually swarms of Kaarrk tactical fighters, so it looks as if the Kaarrk are hauling something enormous into Corduwaine local space. What it might be we cannot guess, except for one theorist at Corduwaine University who has suggested it might be a kind of battery of cosmic proportions that gathers solar energy and discharges it in an enormous pulse that can hurl a destructive cloud of particles light years through bent space at a remote target. Call it long range artillery if you will. For a dissenting view, now hear Dr. Hala Phan of Solar Defense Command."

A woman's voice now sounded. It was a dry, older sounding voice with much authority behind its calm tonality. "The problem with that theory is that we are also seeing Kaarrk command and control cruisers in a lens formation as if guarding this thing. My guess is that it is probably a main, if not the primary, mother ship of the Kaarrk fleet. They feel secure here, having smashed all our defenses. In practical terms, they control Corduwaine space and are now turning it into a strategic stepping stone for a larger attack on the entire humansh defense network across the Rifraf Arm and the Eight Seas of the *Spatium Nostrum*. The question then becomes whether Home

Command can afford to ignore this new behemoth, or if they decide to nuke the entire Corduwaine system, assuming they can still summon that capability amid the ongoing enemy attacks."

I was tempted—*sooo* tempted—to get on the piece and holler at covered with brass to pull back all stray or obsolete units of heroic volunteers. Home space was getting a lot too hot for comfort.

The answer came about eight land hours later, when that same colonel came back on videx to chatter some more. His tone had gone from running narrative to breathless horror. "In huge gulping pulses, this anomaly can surf across parsecs of space in any direction. The Kaarrk have some powerful technologies we can only guess at."

An hour later the colonel broadcast this statement: "Solar Command has now confirmed that the massive object appearing in orbit of our sun is a command and control vessel, not a charge barge or blow and go. We are starting to get ghostly images that appear to show a massive—that is the only word I can think of—maybe behemoth—war ship or war station. It is a huge can of worms, if I may be permitted a bad joke. Their social structure is worm-like, as far as we can tell. They behave like a ball of snakes or worms, synching their cerebral energies. There is some type of hyper-Kaarrk like a queen bee or queen ant or chief worm that focuses their thinking if it can be called thinking. There is a hierarchy of such leader entities or animals that can achieve quick, intelligent focus the way we employ a command hierarchy. They have something like a ring network…"

On it went, and I kept hoping that the 569th was safely back on firm ground.

Then, in the middle of the night, ground time in Corduwaine, came the awful news: "The walls or bulkheads of this behemoth are now materializing out of Temporale space into local space. The mothership of the Kaarrk Swarm is barely a parsec off Tellerine, and not far from Moon 3. Solar Command is desperately casting about for any defensive units still capable of operating. We have been totally devastated.

"Wait, we switch to local videx. A small unit of Civil Defense are on patrol. I hear the local commander ordering them to bail out as fast as possible. They don't stand a chance against the gathering Kaarrk fleet. The support fleet is still hours away as the enormous mothership materializes. Tellerine-based astronomers are scanning the heavens to make visual contact, which is expected in moments as the huge cruiser or flagship dumps out of Temporale space outside time and place."

I was screaming silently inside myself for Zara to get her patrol out of there.

By now the defense grid was locked down and I could not have gotten a command in edgewise had I wanted to. Actually, I wanted to order her back down in the worst way, but I still did not understand the situation in the field.

The colonel kept talking in a dry, journalistic voice: "Six tiny dots—those are the 569th CD scouts led by Reserve Captain Zara Upholder. We have cockpit videx from the wing leader's unit."

The videx showed the inside of Zara's cockpit. You could not tell one suited, booted, helmeted pilot from another, so I had to accept the colonel's word.

A woman's voice cut in: "Wing Leader, this is Ground. Get your holy asses out of there as fast as you can turn those rickety shit crates. That is an order. Now!"

We could not see the women's expressions.

We did see several things.

First, a behemoth wall materialized off Moon 3. The six dots of light were dwarfed. You could make out the surface detail on the Kaarrk mothership, which looked like a vast bronze sphere covered with glyphs and rounded portholes thickly covered in nexglass, a photo-sensitive surface material that relays a photonic image to a screen inside as if there were actually a window in place rather than a meter thick armor plating. You could make out exhaust vents where they blew out toxic by products in little blackish curly streams. You could also make out byflyer drones, those fish-like cleaners and guard scouts that accompany a huge ship like this, the way scavenger fish swim with whales in planetary seas.

"Wing Leader, this is Ground," said that same hoarse female voice. "You are in mortal danger. Bail out now. That is a direct order. You have seconds before those scavenger drones finish you off."

At that moment, the videx clearly showed the two lead pilots—presumably Zara and another woman—briefly linking hands between their seats. Then the lead pilot made that unmistakeable Upholder sign that I'd seen Zara make when she was about to do something dangerous and insane. She raised her arms, with the elbows close together, and the hands raised in a climbing motion. She formed her hands into fists. A quick pan of videx across all six scout craft showed the same gestures being replicated.

Then the image went grainy.

The videx pulled back to the accompanying robot drone, which showed the six scouts one by one hooking toward the mothership rather than away.

One by one, they struck the same point on the hull of the behemoth.

As the final scout struck a weak point they had chosen, a ripple of energy started to run through the hull. We could see it via the drone, before that was blanked out by scavengers, by the energy wave, or by the hull defenses.

My heart was bleak. Zara was dead by then. It was small consolation that the mothership, which was still materializing, was starting to explode in convulsive waves like a puking stomach hurling out its lunch one piccia slice at a time.

The colonel's voice cut back in. He sounded flat and amazed. "We just witnessed the heroic suicide attack by six entities of Tellerine Civil Defense, Unit 569. It appears that the Kaarrk mothership is breaking up. I am receiving word that the energy wave configuration is changing. The escort ships are braking to avoid piling onto the exploding mothership. That means, most likely, they will pull back to regroup—unless they launch a suicide attack on Tellerine, so we need to all hold our breath now and wait for death or survival. I have no idea what their next move will be. I expect to be knocked off system as the implosive self-destruction of this ship, which was as large as a small moon, tears the energy continuum of the entire solar system out of kilter for at least some hours, if not a day or two. Echoes of the explosion will reverb—"

With that, his voice suddenly grew shaky, and the transmission cut out.

As if grieving, the energy grid across all of Tellerine died. The cities grew dark. Engines ceased to chug and thump, causing power outages. All around me, the command center went dark and silent. Even the air in the walls ceased its gentle hissing as it exchanged stale air for fresh. Waves of battered air buffeted in all directions above the city.

There—I could see with the naked eye, looking out through our recently rebuilt windows as a dot of light appeared in space near Moon 3. Like a new star, it raced in all directions, expanding in an ever more rapid explosion that left a dull reddish-bloody ring balefully stretched across millions of miles of open space.

The possible Kaarrk revenge attack did not happen. The enemy support ships withdrew back into extra-solar space. We got word that the Zhar System was sending a fleet of ten destroyers. The Mallik Confederation, both humansh and alienate, was sending a flight of supply vessels. The Sea of Glass command was sending a fleet of hospital ships. The Corsair Nebula (which was neither a nebula nor peopled by pirates) was sending a scout carrier with over 200 shiplets and 10,000 crew. The Union of Argo was sending a flight of stinger jacks, each manned by ten crew, and capable of knocking out a small planet in balls of flame. The Tonton Registry, with sixty independent planetary democracies, was sending a fleet of sixty destroyers and five heavy battle cruisers. And so it went, one by one, as word came in that the galaxy of ManTime, the reborn universe, had decided that the ultra-alien nature of the Kaarrk was too far beyond any reasonable moral boundary even for the strangest of our new alien allies.

For my part, I ignored an imperious, almost hysterial holog from Trask himself.

The Upholder had something important to say to me—no, to yell in my face—and I wasn't having any of it.

My mind was on a summer garden on Tulearth, where I was a young man wearing only a loincloth, hoeing rich humus filled with flowers. The air smelled of blossoms and flittered with butterflies. A beautiful young woman with the styling of a princess, the beauty of a mythic fae, the lithe grace of an Amazon, and the mischief of a garden elf glided toward me on sun-tanned toes under a wind-blown garment of colorful gauze that just revealed the caramel skin on her lithe limbs…

My life on Tellerine was finished. Like the young man in the song, I wanted to leave Galata for the open countryside, where the air was thin and pure. I longed to hear the birds, *kushlar*, singing on the wires, *telgrafin tellerine*, all down the road to freedom. I was done here. I had lost everything.

So I stole an air skimmer and streaked away, just as the first lights began to glimmer back across the city grid, and normalcy was starting to show its promise.

Someone tried to raise me on the videx, but I tore the wires out from under the dashboard.

Nothing would ever be normal or right for me again. My heart had been torn out of my chest, my soul out of my life.

Only the mysterious and magical force of life and survival, burned into the instincts of our inner wires, kept me from achieving orbital speed and then streaking straight down into the earth to end it all in one instant, as Zara had done, but in my case for no purpose.

Or I could achieve orbital velocity, then escape velocity, and streak out into open space toward Moon 3 and join Zara and the other heroes. I could imagine what she would say, and kept on straight out toward the starfield.

Chapter 7. Galata

Streaking toward Upholder space port (what other name would it have on this world?), I noticed a faint light far behind me.

Flying level at 300 meters, I noticed a strobing light, tiny at first, but rapidly gaining on me. I saw also the coppery glow of afterburners, and recognized the red-white-blue alert flashers of a police skimmer. No way would I outrun that guy. I felt so beaten that I did not have the energy, even in my rage and loss, even with tears streaming across my cheeks like rain, to try.

The police flier streaked past me and got in front of me with his lights and flashers making a circus. Rather than ram him—or her—I slowed down, matching his pace, until we were stopped in midair.

Oddly, it was a gray cruiser with red markings on its sides and rear—not a regular airways police patrol. Displayed in the air above and around the cruiser were white letters that read *HM Sacred Agent. Pull over—Police or Emergency Official Business. You will be cited if you do not comply.*

As I waited—drying my tear-blinded face with an airweave towel—a quadrille *faux* floor appeared in mid-air under both vehicles. Doors opened ahead of me, and two persons stepped out. The driver, on the right, was a dark-blond man in gray clothing—a uniformed agent of the spiritual authority, kind of rare to see doing traffic duty, so this must be something much more. The passenger on the left was Zara, getting out in tight black garments. Both wore dark glasses whose impersonal looking lenses flashed with reflected flasher lights.

The male agent waited by the cruiser, while the military priestess slowly approached my car. Both persons carefully palmed their side arms, ready to draw if I were someone other than they expected.

I was so taken back that for a moment, in my grief and hope, I believed she was Zara. My lost love, hero of the nation. I loved her more than I loved my own life. I faced the woman coming toward me with a reckless, unfeeling courage like nothing I had ever experienced. I had learned it from Zara.

She walked more quickly as she saw I was really Ranay Fennelon. She removed her glasses and twirled them in one strong caramel-colored hand (just like Zara's). *Remarkable.* I was breathless.

"Ranay."

I croaked: "Zara." Had she come back from the dead?

"No, my name is Araz. I am your wife's twin sister."

She leaned on the window well of my car with black-clad arms. Her beautiful face was within arm's length of mine. Where Zara had carried with her a faint scent of sweet soaps and flowery perfume, this woman had more an aroma of forest floors, army tents, and gun oil. Her hands were faintly scarred from fighting, unlike Zara's smooth custard skin. Her fingers looked rough, her nails broken and plain unlike Zara's pink or honey daubs depending on the mood and the occasion. She tapped her fingers business-like on the ceramic auto skin. "Nice to meet you, brother."

"I didn't know Zara had another sister."

"We are—were—twins fathered by Trask with the same mother, rest her soul. Zara never mentioned me, by my request. I found my calling in service of the Holy Mother when we were little girls. Zara never understood, but she respected." She looked me over, with my bulging eyes and gaping mouth. "We will not meet again when these days are past," she said. "I am about to follow my calling to a distant assignment on another world in another system."

I managed to begin speaking. "I thought you were Zara."

"I know. We were born identical sisters—naturally, not by gene-engineer tricks. We loved each other very much. She went one way, and I went the other. I would give anything to trade places with her. I was supposed to be the fighter, and she the lover. So it turns out we are twins again—both fighters. I can never save an entire civilization, as she did, but I am proud of her."

"So am I."

"I know. That is why she sent me."

"She." It was a question.

She stared at me and clicked those broken nails on my car window again. She looked at me with serious, liquid-thoughtful eyes in a beautiful face, which however was empty of the love I had known in Zara's features. Same strong jaw, wide expressive mouth, streamlined nose. "You were leaving, huh?"

"I am."

"Well, then I won't stop you."

"But you already have." I was getting my senses back, and with them the same bravado as when I'd first met Zara. It was almost the same meeting again, except there was no love. But we had Zara in common, and that made us family. She was my sister. I suddenly had lost a love and gained a sister.

"I just thought I'd meet you one time before you leave us forever." She twirled her dark eye gear confrontationally.

I changed the subject. I didn't want to leave (yet). "You're on official business." It was another question.

She twirled her glasses toward the waiting agent. "That's a very official car. Yes, you could say so."

"Am I under arrest?"

She seemed surprised. "You are free to go." She stepped back. "Go."

I sat staring at her. "I could have had this conversation with your sister. I know exactly where it's going. You have my attention. So spill the beans."

She regarded me with a look that was like a river flowing with a jumble of dark, mixed thoughts. I detected a trace of uncertainty. Of course I did. I had been intimate with her twin sister. They were duplicate stanzas of the same pavane. I understand Araz better than she understood me, even with Zaraesque genes.

"Choices," she said carefully. "If you have made up your mind, just go. Get out of here."

"I'm not leaving. I have nowhere to go. I'm running away."

"You're honest. That's promising."

"I am pulling teeth with you."

She surrendered, folding her shades and slipping them in to an ammo pocket in her black rack. "Very well, Ranay. Would you maybe stay here?"

"If I could stand the pain, maybe."

"You will be in more pain if you leave here."

"I'm not sure." I added: "Yes. You're right, of course."

We stared at each other, two honest souls, a brother and sister. Would I long to return to the place where I loved and lost? Would I take the vapur back to Galata? Or would I follow the telegrafin tellerine down that endless road into a future that would never again bring me down this way? What did that unknown young man have to return to—a mountain village smelling of cow crap?

Araz leaned in, knowing she had almost closed her sale. She tapped her chipped nails on the car and looked at me, her eyes mildly brimming with bravado and triumph.

"You win," I said. "What is my other option? Something to do with Trask? The Church? What?" I should have asked: Who sent you? Who *really* sent you?

"All of the above."

"Shine a light, sister."

She touched me—for the first and last time in this way. She laid a hard, sweet hand with boyish fingers on my arm. She gripped my arm with the force of her emotions, so that those fingernails turned white and bluish. "Brother."

I reached out and put my hand over hers. She felt warm, and vulnerable. She was giving her heart to me, in the only way a military priestess under vows of poverty, chastity, and obedience ever could to a man. I squeezed her hand and rocked it gently.

"Trask," she said, swallowing with emotion, and there was a wetness about her large, dark eyes, "my father, a thorough bastard but loveable man who has done only good for all his children, sent me with a message."

"And that is?"

"I have already delivered it. I am the message."

"Spell it out. I'm a little slow."

"Follow us."

I sat gaping again while she strode away, her shoulders high, and her head hunched down between them. I watched her shadowy, shapely form stride away. I would only see her once more, at least now, in this life, how things were to turn out.

She got back into the car, as did the Sacred Agent. The lights and sirens turned off. The fake road quadrille winked out of existence. Two doves fluttered past, rising obliquely as if the plane had never been there. A moment earlier, they would have bumped their heads. I followed the cruiser's amber backlights in a long U-turn that took us back into the city, past Upholder Starfield, toward the family's central compound that sprawls over acres in the northern range of Corduwaine. It is a marvel of white and gilded domes (the Holy Mother's colors of state, come to think of it). There are blue pools, green orchards, brick walks, white walls, glass-green windows. It is where Trask reigned as chief of the Upholder clan and political boss of Tellerine, head of the clans, capo of all the capi in the planet's Nostra Causa. The causa has a bloody history, but it's all for a bona causa so to speak. Tellerine, when not blasted by aliens, has a solid economy, a large equestrian or artisan middle class, and no starving underthanes on her streets. People like

Trask run it with a steel hand, which does not seem attractive to the milder sorts of folks, but the Holy Mother and her abbesses and amazons bring balance. Never mind a long discussion—it works for what it's worth. What was it worth to me? A lot, apparently. I followed Araz and the time traveler back to the estate, where Trask himself welcomed me as his only surviving son—and heir.

Long story short, I stayed. Highlights I'll tell you just the following.

Last time I would ever see my newly found sister, we stood together with other dignitaries of Tellerine around the portable throne of the Holy Mother. The aliens never got this. They thought we were worms like them. Decapitate us by taking out our leader, and we shriveled into a pile of husks. Wrong. There are as many Holy Mothers as we need to carry the word of Peace and Love around the ManTime galaxy. We've learned our lessons about arrogance, bullying, and all that.

Holy Mother Menemet VI died with her generals and attendants when the Kaarrk Swarm struck. What the Kaarrk Swine could not know was that at the moment Menemet VI expired in a volcano of flames and bombs, which turned to glass the Blue Sea Bay of Lue, the next Holy Mother woke far, far away from a normal night's sleep as a crowd of abbesses, military priestesses, and augurs blew open the doors of her bed chamber and rushed in to announce that she was now the spiritual leader of all human kind. Word travels fast on the spirit network. Seventy light years away, on a pinkish sand planet in the Sea of Marigold Fields, in a cloister of sugar-white pillars and pollen-yellow domes, an ordinary *epi-skopia* went to bed thinking of nothing but her quiet prayers and maybe the accounts of her store rooms and the care of sixty or so nuns under her oversight. By morning she had been announced by the universal Church as Menemet VII, Holy Mother of all humankind. So after the Swine were smashed and driven away, there was a great celebration among the human, humansh, humanoid, humanish, and off-alien peoples who would have rather died entirely rather than become garbage for the Kaarrk maggots to creep and wriggle around in. Thousands of worlds celebrated across the galaxy as the Kaarrk were driven back into the far Sea of Fear. There would be many Swarm wars and battles yet, but the worst had been averted.

One day not long after, Holy Mother Menemet VII and a fleet of powerful battleships appeared out of Temporale space to honor the twelve maidens of Tellerine who had saved the universe. As Holy Mother was brought to Corduwaine to honor us all, Trask and his clan (and I) were ushered into Her holy presence in the great cathedral of the local *episkopa* or overseer. All the clans were represented, and all the leaders were there in a semicircle on a red carpet around the throne, which rose three man-heights above us on fragrant honeywood scented with jasmine and incense. The new Holy Mother was still young and pretty, not at all adorned with rouges, powders, or shadowliners as is the style for secular women. She wore the gilded robes and head dress, and wielded the long, slender twin scepters of civil and spiritual authority in white-gloved hands. The usual bands played, and organ music blasted us with harmonious oceans of sound. Then it grew silent so you could only hear the echoes of coughing, feet shuffling, chairs scraping on the stone tile floors of the high basilica with its floating stained-glass windows. As always, Her throne was surrounded by squads of black-clad military priestesses. We still feared Kaarrk assassins, as Trask privately told me, so the precautions were extraordinary, but She demanded and commanded to be seen among the people. She was ready to live or die, as her predecessor had been, because in a soul's moment, another woman could awaken somewhere in the galaxy and become the next Holy Mother, servant of the servants of the divine.

In that crowd were my own family from Luxanne: my father Vilo, a self-made and wealthy agricultural domineer; my mother Istha who taught mathematics at the Uni; my brother Manil, a planet-building terraformer; and my sisters Livin and Haril, still studying to be professors. They stood proudly together, and I exchanged many fond looks with them across the sea of faces.

Trask made me stand on one side of him, and Araz on the other. Every clan had at least one daughter or sister who belonged to holy orders, so this was all true to form. We were a wall of gray and maroon and forest green and marbled and mustard yellow leggins and blousets and puffy elbow or shoulder joints as the fashion of the day ran. Men generally wore shiny dark blue or green suede berets with decorative plumes, while women wore pleated kilts of all sorts of dignified designs, and gray leggins and high, graceful riding boots. Amid all the speeches and songs and dances occurred the following exchange.

"We are pleased to meet the families of the Twelve Women," said the Holy Mother in a clear, strong voice that echoed like glass being carefully stacked or cut. She looked down at me and Trask and Araz. The Holy Mother was strong and brave. "We send treasures from the galaxy to fund a magnificent obelisk already designed, which will bear on it the names of the Twelve Saints, and a motto to be chosen by the ruling council of Tellerine." She regarded Araz. "And this priestess is the sister of my beloved Zara." It was a question.

Araz turned red and bowed awkwardly, looking almost mannish in her black jack and weaponry.

"Henceforth, my child, you will bear the name Zaraz or Zararaz in honor of our dear sister, your twin. You will now carry both your names."

Trask nudged his daughter, and she blurted: "Yes ma'am. Thank you." She was not good with ceremonies.

I didn't blame Araz or Zararaz. I thought my own skin was afire, so afraid was I that the Holy Mother would speak to me next. Which she did soon enough.

"You are Zara's beloved."

"Yes, Holy Mother," I managed to say.

"I am told you are now a member of her family, by marriage as well as by common sacrifice and loss."

"Yes, Holy Mother."

She turned her face slightly toward Trask, who stood beside me. As she spoke, I noticed that she moved her twin scepters in slight, heavily significant ceremonial gestures. One was close to the heart, an the other upraised like a sword. The augurs know and record the symbolism in her every gesture. I only knew she was pleased. Divine help us all if she were not pleased. "You are Upholder," she said.

He, tightening his steel grip unexpectedly on my neck, said: "I am Trask, Holy Mother. I am old and tired, a broken man full of grief. I have here beside me the Upholder." With that, his steel fingers tightened briefly on my neck. I thought he would snap my vertebrae. Instead, he released his grip and stepped back. A gasp went through the entire cathedral. Even the Holy Mother lowered her twin scepters to her lap, and her mouth opened in shock. Trask had just shot a hole in the etiquette, the protocol, and the schedule of ceremonies. Trask had been designated along with Zararaz to light a torch to some sort of ceremonial flame that would burn for the rest of time on the grave site of Holy Mother Menemet VI on the Bay of Lue. Now what was this all about?

My knees shook as trumpets (haut-boys) resounded in clarion harmony under the stained glass images of past Tellerine rulers and episkopai and all sorts of cherubs and alienoid figments.

"Upholder!" a man someplace shouted.

"Upholder!" came the cry from a dozen throats, then a hundred, a thousand.

"Upholder," said the Holy Mother. She raised her twin scepters parallel together like pillars in a temple entrance.

Hands pushed me so I stumbled forward. Zararaz took me by one elbow, and Trask by the other, as they led me closer to the foot of the throne. Menemet VII slowly climbed down, aided by a dozen military priestesses and gray-clad sacred agents (men and women). The popess stood on the lowest rung of the throne while her chamberlain (an elderly man who looked like a wizard with a long gray beard) whispered in her ear. That would be Mr. Protocol, or Sir Merlin, or whatever. She was a creature of ceremony, and nodded, taking charge in an instant. She knew what to do.

"Ranay Fennelon of Luxanne."

"Yes, Holy Mother."

I trembled, as Zararaz and Trask continued to hold me by the elbows, lest I fall down in a faint.

She lowered both scepters to touch my shoulders. "I greet you as the new Upholder. From now on, you will be Ranay Trask Upholder, by the will and testament of your father in law, Upholder Trask of Tellerine. You are now chieftain of the Clan Upholder, chief of council, magistrate of Corduwaine, and my primary civil judge in the Corduwaine system. Welcome to our service."

"I am honored," I said, "*Bla bla bla*" or syllables to that effect. Lots of them, until my mouth (soon) ran dry and nothing more came out.

Zararaz embraced me briefly. Her job was done. For just an instant, holding her form in my hands was a faint echo of how it felt to hold Zara. She planted a single dry kiss on my cheek, and walked away with other military priestesses. She cast one last, fond look back at me. She walked out of my life forever as Zara had done. I am occasionally briefed on her good works as an abbess and later an *episkopa* in the distant Bell Flower system in the Sea of Autumn Leaves in the Rifraf Arm. I watched the amber glow of her cars and companions recede into distance and destiny. How could anyone know, back then, that she was destined to become the Holy Mother Menemet VIII one day, and sit with her sister and me overlooking the mournful but triumphant celebrations of our holy martyrs at the Bay of Lue on the Sea of Blue?

How short our lives are, and how vast is this space in which we dwell. What a great cathedral it is, the cosmos, in which the echoes of our tiny voices quickly fade to nothing. New voices arise, however briefly, and think they are the only ones who have tasted moon berries or breathed in the young summer wind. How quickly their moment passes, and yet it is the supreme of all events. There is glory in that.

The hall filled with roaring voices and a thunder of applauding hands. The rest of that day followed in a swirl of cyclonic emotions and barely remembered moments. I remember we had a great feast and I ate well.

I have dictated my memoirs, which are stored in the official libraries of Tellerine. The other story I must tell is about moon berries.

Chapter 8. Upholder

Not long after I became Upholder, and Trask had retired to a sunny island to spend his remaining years at play, I was told by an aide that a visitor awaited me in the great library of Upholder House.

It was Trask, but that is not really the story. He looked tanned and rested. He looked fit and relaxed. Gone was the bluster. He said to me, standing among leatherette globes and expensive show books amid dim garnet lights and green dots and all manner of tellerine wiring: "You look well, my boy."

"Thank you, Trask." I could not bring myself to call him father, since a man can only have one father, and my dear father was back on Luxanne with my family, living their lives out as if I were still away at university, not de facto ruler of a planet.

"You have another choice to make," said he as he held a handful of figs in one hand, and popped one into his mouth with the other. "I envy you."

"I am honored," I said. I should have said I was confused, which was more the truth. What could the old goat have up his sleeve now? What joke, what trick, what horror was he about to play on me? A planet lived in dread of him, even now that he had retreated to the windy western islands (and no small number of attractive women, wine bearers, and so forth).

Trask signaled for me to follow him. Still juggling figs in one hand, and a wine chalice in the other, he led me across luxurious carpets, through halls jammed with hazy lighting and digital spiderwebbing, to a side hall. The room was large, and empty. Its floors were thickly carpeted in a kind of rich, chewy array of forest golds and browns mingled with glass-green and claret red hues. Trask stopped, so that I bumped into him from behind. He said: "I don't know how much longer I have on this world. You are the Upholder now, and soon will be the next Trask. Fate took my sons, but gave me you. My sweet girl is gone, and my other child is married to my life's worst mistake, miserable Sender. She would have been good for you also. By the rights and customs of Tellerine, and our family, I give you a choice you can either take or leave. I will not hold it against you if you say no."

Puzzled, I took a playful air. "You won't threaten to toss me out of a window?"

He guffawed. "I don't have the strength anymore. Nor the rage. I am spent." He pointed a fig in my face. "You, on the other hand, are young and better educated than I ever was. You have been a military cadet, and you understand discipline and, by the Holy Mother, all that kindness and crap that I never found time for. You will take the Upholder name up a notch or two. Make us elegant again, like we were before my time. I have one more treasure to give you."

With that, he pushed open a double door, and we emerged on a balcony overlooking the Blue Sea. The glassy death lake that had been the Bay of Lue spread before us. A newly built obelisk rose into a yellow-reddish evening sun like a needle about to pierce a star. Ocean water flooded the glassy bay a fathom deep, cooling it enough so people could soon be able to walk on it.

Trask said: "Ask me, and I will say yes."

I had no idea what he meant.

With that, he turned abruptly, in his characteristic huff, and stalked away, disappearing into the empty carpeted hall. He closed the double doors, leaving me alone on the balcony with the evening sun.

For a moment, I stood alone and confused. Then I became aware of the woman standing near the balcony. *Artemi.* She had grown up. I had not seen her in months. The loss of her sister, the deaths of thousands, the destruction of her home and city, the shock of war, had changed her forever. She had become a woman and more so, an Upholder.

"Hello, Ranay."

"Artemi." Saying her name was like having the golden sun in my mouth. I swallowed hard.

She strode toward me as Zara had, years earlier, in the garden on Tulearth. She was tall, and sure, with long legs and neatly square toes. She wore a long white gown that billowed gently in the warm evening air, dimly hinting at the delicious shapes moving underneath. She was an Upholder. There was no question. Everything about her, from her hair to her eyes, from her mouth to her jaw, from her long neck to her small, high breasts under that sheer garment, spoke of majesty and grace.

"I have a gift for you if you will take it, Ranay."

I had difficulty speaking. "I know what your father meant. I am honored beyond words."

She was that gift.

She came directly to me and put her hands on my chest. If I said no, she would push herself away, like a swimmer in the ocean turning toward a distant island under screaming gulls. I felt a trembling in her hands, a flutter like wings, *kushlar*, birds. Dear, beloved soul.

My eyes spoke first, when my mouth could not, a song of songs: *You are beautiful, my love, like an army under way with flying banners. You are powerful, like a storm under heaven.*

The blind poet of long-ago Earth might have written in a margin of the epics: A ewe, stalked by the shepherd, darts left and right. It finally stops with pleading in its honeyed eyes, but sees love and mercy in his open hands. It will graze upon the hunter's meadows and want for nothing.

I surrender to your will; my heart rejoices in captivity. Let us run on the meadows together as the shining sun swims among the planets.

Her fists closed around my shirt. She pulled me toward her, while I put my arms around her willowy figure.

"Say it," she commanded. The trembling, the flutter, vanished.

"Yes."

She put her arms roughly around my neck. We pulled together in one motion. She kissed me—her response to my answer. I tasted summer and honey as I overpowered her with my desire. Somehow, that awkward child had known, long ago, that she and I were destined to be sun and moon.

Soon after this, she formally became the wife of my life, the woman standing with me at the ceremonies overlooking the Bay of Lue by the

Sea of Blue, surrounded by our children, as we watch the 569th ceremonial marathon marchers link arms between throne and obelisk while all the sad, weeping bands of the galaxy slowly play the Tellerine anthem in memory of Zara and the other saints and martyrs. What must our sister Zararaz be feeling as she sits in splendor behind us, out of reach in her majesty, yet so near to us as one heart is to another—my sister, the twin of lost Zara, blood sister of Artemi, daughter of Trask, child of Tellerine and Corduwaine, now the most sacred vessel of all humankind.

That evening years earlier, on the balcony of Trask's palace, we gladly sealed our fate as it was meant to be. Artemi's blue eyes shone like stars, a breath away from my face, and looking deep into my eyes. I had answered her most pressing question: *yes*.

Raising glasses of moon berry wine, we interlocked our arms to drink in our new and eternal union. Looking into each other's eyes, we recited together as one, in a quiet, firm voice meant to resonate forever: "I love you more than I love my own life."

Ten Years Later

Chapter 9. Kushlar

As Lord and Trask of Corduwaine, Master of the World, I was expected to take my wife and children to our annual victory and independence celebrations in the Bay of Lue by the Sea of Blue.

At this moment, a few hundred special guests were on the high bleachers overlooking thousands on the plain below. A reddish sunset wallowed amid dusky, sweet clouds in the peaceful atmosphere. Fliers of all types, with winking belly and tail lights, nuzzled in the clouds looking down with videx and glittering windows. The sacred avenue stretched a ceremonial mile across the glassy plain from the Holy Mother's throne to the darkly, tragically looming obelisk that recorded our deadly struggle for existence not so many years earlier.

"Lord Trask," a young military priestess or MP in black combat gear addressed me without ceremony or due respect. "The Holy Mother requires your presence."

The MP popped up so suddenly at my side that I nearly jumped out of my skin. They are not required to stand on ceremony, these young women who with their lives guard the Holy Mother, civil and spiritual leader of all humankind across the seas and arms of the galaxy.

The young priestess's tone conveyed—*immediately, if not sooner.*

The unnamed young military priestess, who spoke with a slight offworld accent, had mussy blond hair, a bruised face, taped grimy knuckles, and a frayed tunic. She wore a dagger in her belt, and a compact side arm strapped to the other side. Her brown eyes were large, direct, and expecting no questions. The Holy Mother's word has absolute authority, on my world and all others. Thousands of celebrants around me were dressed in their finest, washed, and perfumed. Not these holy fighters, dressed almost in rags, who are of this world, and yet not.

I exchanged looks with my wife, who apparently knew something I didn't. So I nodded to the MP and said: "We'll follow you."

She stepped back like a black shadow, impatiently awaiting that I—and my family—would immediately follow her. She raised her wrist to speak into a com bracelet with her companions. Security was tight, extending across this parade, and the city, and far across the Corduwaine system for our all-important guest, the Popess, who had just oddly summoned us to Her august presence. I had no idea what was about to happen.

My tall young wife, finely dressed for this occasion of state, wearing a gauzy white gown and velvety black wrap, nodded while giving me a significant look I did not yet fully understand. "We are coming along," she said brightly. She took the hands of our two smaller boys, twins, while my older daughter took the little girls in tow. We followed the young military priestess through the crowd of festive citizens, who politely made way amid their excitement as they prepared to see marching bands, floats, patriotic units, passing flyers in review.

I had no idea of the surprise that lay in store.

This was the annual celebration of our desperate victory a decade earlier against an enemy so alien that hatred would be a kind word to describe their attitude toward humankind. Hatred would be an emotion, casually cited, but not really meaningful since the Kaarrk Swarm have no individuality—just numbers, and merciless hive-drive. They long only to kill and destroy. If they die in combat, their final and only emotion is rage that they will no longer be able to hate. You see the terror of our situation not long ago, and the miracle of our victory.

As we followed the MP across the high celebrity platform, we were surrounded by thousands of Corduwaine system and Tellerine world dignitaries and citizens. A man and woman alternated echoing commentaries in excited voices on loud-vox brayers, and occasional thumping of military music rose into the food-scented air. The atmosphere was by parts carnival, solemn, and get-together.

I was not born here, but I became a leading citizen. It would not be out of place for me to be summoned to see the Holy Mother in person. The timing was simply off, and I felt puzzled. But the Holy Mother says come, you go, no questions. Local dignitaries were supposed to meet with the spiritual and civil leader of humankind tomorrow in ceremonies in the city. The Popess had come in a convoy of warships to attend our celebration and honor the many who died defending humankind on the battlefield below, where the Kaarrk had launched the first of their savage surprise assaults—but we defeated them at such heart-wrenching cost.

I was once a young man from a simple place—a planet that hurtles around a yellow sun, much as folks say said old mythic Earth once did, if she ever really existed, and perhaps still does somewhere in fathomless space. Named Ranay by my parents, I was their first-born—smart, handsome, and ambitious. I was chosen by my *deme*, and my parents sent me to the fabulous university on Tulearth in the Corduwaine system, light years from home. The plan was for me to become a skilled starmansh, an officer, and a doctor among the stars, so I could return home and serve my people. As fate would have it, my future was written in a very different book. Nobody can go back and change time. I will tell you how those things came to be, and you must promise not to cry.

In a moment, I will tell you how I first met Zara Upholder of Tellerine in the Corduwaine system. First, I must describe how we live today, especially in that we will never forget. When I am done telling, this story will make sense.

We are at peace now, at a terrifying price of blood and death in years past. Sleeping amid the ages, across from me on this parade field, are the truncated and battered pyramid ruins of ghostly Fortress Mercury. They loom in a fog of distance and evening, under a sprinkling of fiery pinpricks in a cloud-feathered sky over the skyline of Corduwaine, capital city of Tellerine, chief residence of our House Upholder. Every year at this time, tears come to my eyes as I stand behind the high barriers with my wife and children, watching military priestesses and other officials below in their solemn independence parades. The ceremonies are staged on the battle-blasted glass of a lost bay—under the distant memorial of a far more ancient war. Fortress Mercury's massive walls are worn down by the winds and rains of thousands of years, and full of scars and holes of ancient wars long before our time or memory. Like the glassy plain of Lue, those walls signal to heaven and earth that it is ManTime, and we are still here. We prevailed, but at what cost.

On Tellerine in the Corduwaine system, years are phased much like those on mythical Old Earth. Each summer, on an easy warm dusk like this, I bring my family to the dry, glass-blasted Bay of Lue on the Sea of Blue for our annual remembrance celebrations. If only we could roll back time without destroying the universe, what would I give—or would I—to change anything? Life has been good after all, despite war and loss. We slowly grow older, and many of the thousands who stand solemnly around us were not born yet during the terror and the Swarm attacks, which changed everything—so long ago. We are the older ones, honored ones, who stand on the highest ramps to watch the ceremonies in the crater below. Our children had not yet come into this world, but they stand with us now.

Picture us on such an evening, among many thousands, as the military priestess arrives to summon us. I have one of my daughters on my shoulders—the littlest, who is still light enough to be carried so. Beside me stands my oldest, the daughter who looks so much like her mother and her mother's sister Zara that my heart aches every time I see this child. She keeps one smooth, caramel hand with happily, seductively painted pink nails on the unruly hair of my twin boys who make up the middle children. On the steel railing before me sits my oldest son, who is now twelve. My wife stands behind him, holding her arms around his waist to steady him (and rest herself). He is a strapping young boy with forest-dark hair. It is Upholder hair. Trask is long dead and gone, his ashes peacefully enurned at the foot of the obelisk. My son has intelligent eyes and a straight back, and will most likely serve in the Defense Fleets a generation from now. Rulership, military service, and sometimes the ultimate sacrifice are in Upholder family genes. I married into their clan, welcomed by the late, powerful Lord Upholder who governed cities, plantations, mountains, and vast bodies of water, all under the roiling golden-red clouds of Tellerine.

It is a planet named for pioneering signal wires, in an ancient Earth language known as Haegean—nobody remembers for sure, and the ancient syllables are garbled, but the emotional story is crystal clear as if told today. The story is also known as the Wisdom of Birds (*kushlar*). There is a story, sung by griots along far Temporale rail lines and on nexus starways, about a naïve young country lad who left his home village and went to a big city. It is a song of Old Earth, full of sadness, loss, and freedom. The young man had foolishly lost his heart to a beautiful young courtesan, or *hypnodoule*, in Old Galata, where money and sex flowed like honey, and a fool from the farm could get cleaned out in a few days. Having lost at love and life, the young man walks away from the city (legendary Stamboule) with a heavy heart, but his steps grow lighter with every mile he puts between himself and desires lost. He vows never to return, not to take a *vapuret* ferry across the Dolemoon river (the ancient words are garbled in folk memory). It is a story universal to humankind; our people, who have suffered much since our fall from arrogance, understand it instantly across eons and starways. As he walks on a road to freedom from smothering city to that fresh country air he can breathe more easily, the young man sees how life and time roll on. There is always healing from even the worst suffering. He envies the birds who sit on ancient copper *telgrafin* wires (*tellerine*) above his head, free from gravity and cares. The birds (*kushlar*) twitter endlessly in a language without words, but full of feelings. We don't need to know who the boy was, or what the birds twittered among each other, or what exactly happened in the city among the doules; we can rather imagine that they continued plying their music and their wiles with painted eyes and rouged lips. The ancient song does not tell us in words, nor does it need to. Rather, it sings to us across whispering light years and oceans of stardust, of people like us long ago who lived and died, but they lived lives just as we do, and we remember them through their songs. Our heartbeats and feelings flow together millennia later. Eons from now, when we are dust and forgotten, others of our kind will remember these songs as if they happened only yesterday. That is our humansh strength, which the Kaarrk never could understand in their hate and destructiveness.

Those of us today standing on the high honor-ramps lived during the surprise ambush that started a massive war spanning stars and seas of stars. Where once Kaarrk Swarm buzzers and cutters streaked through the atmosphere, sowing thunder and flames, death and horror, today only colored bubbles and balloons rise playfully on a peaceful summer night's breeze. Solemn music rises, along with the fragrance of smoldering incense in crystal lanterns.

This evening of remembrances, the spiritual and civil ruler of all humankind has come to offer respects. The Holy Mother sits enthroned on a high platform, surrounded by magnificent banners and flags, as well as a large retinue. She holds the twin slender ivory scepters of her sway—the one civil, the other spiritual. She is surrounded by battalions of military priestesses, as well as sacred agents, our own Civil Defense in uniform, and citizen families dressed in their finest. The sacred agents, male and female, wear drab, but the uniform of the military priestesses is black as night—right as might, all tight and fight—including high boots and short tunics with hoods thrown back, with daggers and pistols on their matte web belts; on fluttering pennants held high, their totem bird is the crow, color of night, smart and deadly, a sephir of the Holy Wisdom.

So then comes the surprise, and you will understand this shortly, in due time, for I promise to make this story no longer than your patience will hold out. When we arrived at the throne of Menemet VIII, I felt a shudder of surprise. I had not realized who she was, this sister of us all. The woman sitting on the throne was special—heart of my heart, skin of my skin, eyes of my soul. I had not realized that there was a new popess in the Rifraf Arm, Sea of Colored Glass, in whose stellar clouds which Tellerine world and Corduwaine system are but glimmering atoms among the myriad. Life made all the more sense now. Surrounded by her fighting men and women, the sacred agents and military priestesses, the sister of humankind, servant of the servants of the divine, was a study in reserve and majesty. I genuflected before her. She barely moved her eyes, but I read the emotions roiling behind all that reserve and majesty. My wife and elder daughters brought my family to their knees around me. The woman sitting above us, with her twin scepters and regalia of power, looked upon us with god-love. There was an expression in her eyes as ancient and powerful as the long history of humankind. Her love for us all was our starlight and sunlight. It was no longer personal. It was about our entire race, and its existence, and its rightful but peaceful place in the universe. The assembled mix of important humansh, manoid, alienian, and other dignitaries on the platforms beyond her testified to how we had together made peace, and driven the Kaarrk back to their corner of hell with the promise: *Never Again Like This*, meaning the thousands of names on the obelisk that we honored this evening.

When the music of massed marching corps rose from below to summon our attention, we stepped to the railings near the Holy Mother, and looked down as special ceremonies began on the plain, on the Bay of Lue at the Sea of Blue.

It is the historical privilege of Tellerine's 569th Civil Defense Squadron to lead these rituals, in remembrance of the twelve saints whose names are engraved on the memorial, along with the names of 10,000 martyrs. The marchers forming up far below are all women, wearing distinctive gray-and-maroon battle fatigues. With shouted commands, their line surges forward. They have a unique marching style for this one special event. Three hundred form a wide crescent across the avenue by linking their arms over their neighbors' shoulders for the heroes' walk. This will take them along the sacred way, across the glassy ground that was once the Bay of Lue, toward a towering obelisk. The scarred face of the valley says it all. It was not long ago a fiery battlefield on which a former popess and her generals died. The former ocean bay now reveals a mottled glass surface that is solid and inset with white impactor splashes. On the obelisk, which rises into blood-red, plasma-yellow sunset clouds, are inscribed the names of ten thousand martyrs, among them our twelve saints.

The specially chosen 300 inheritors of the 569th CDS battle unit form a tightly linked line across the avenue. They push their shoulders eagerly forward while holding each other. They thrust their chins forward, as if seeking a fight, while they pull each other forward and support each other. They march slowly and gracefully in unity, with high-kicking steps. Each has a lamplight embedded in the point of each boot-toe. In unison, 300 lights slowly rise while another 300 lights fall, and they do this in perfect cadence to show the strength of the one out of many. The distance from Holy Mother's throne to the obelisk is a ceremonial mile of 3000 such steps.

Accompanying the march is a slow, solemn rendition of a primordial song of Old Earth, *Telgrafin Tellerine*, played with mournful dignity by the massed bands and pipe corps of all Tellerine and Corduwaine military units. These bands stand in cloud-like arrays across the dusky lake bed, with their helmets gleaming in the evening sun, and their cloaks rippling in a gentle breeze. They leave clear a straight path (the *Sacra Via*) between throne and obelisk, after kneeling before the Holy Mother for Her blessing. The popess, in all her majesty, looks distant and tiny in her golden vestments and peaked crown; she watches with intent stillness while holding twin ivory scepters crossed over her heart.

The known galaxy is filled with our kind, though the Swarm and the Inversion have tried to kill us off. We will never go away. Our song will never end. That is the meaning of the solemn march of the young cadets holding each other by the shoulders in solidarity. They slowly high-step across the lake bed with rising and falling stars before their toes to guide them. Above all, the military priestesses and sacred agents do not fear death in the great Nostra Causa.

Holy Mother has traveled here to bless these sacred rites. We will never forget. That is our promise to Her, and to the ten thousand names on the obelisk. *Numquam Hac*—Never Again Like This—reads the legend on the Bay of Lue in the Sea of Blue.

This night, more than ever, tears stream down my eyes—and my wife's—as we think of those who are gone so that we may live, and we think of who the woman is on the throne behind us, the new servant of the servants of the divine, sister of all humankind.

= ***Fin*** =

Author Info

John T. Cullen, a San Diego Author

More info about all this on my webplex. See:

www.sandiegoauthor.com

and

www.johntcullen.com

among other sites on my webplex online.

======

I've been online a quarter century (since 1996) and continue building a webplex of thematically linked websites.

For this story, and many others I have written, please visit the Clocktower Books website at www.clocktowerbooks.com.

Seventy+ novels, short stories, and poetry collections can be found linked on my webplex online

Other features include my online shopping mall, with stylish Citta Moda (www.cittamoda.com) and more stuff coming. I also showcase all things Paris and Parisian at my Paris Bookshop (www.parisbookshop.com) so please do visit. There is a lot to browse, and you can support the effort by buying something through the affiliate retail links online.

Thanks, and enjoy the reading!

Sample My Work Online:

Read over a million words of my fiction, nonfiction, and poetry *free* at

www.galleycity.com

Read Half Free/Try-Buy. Best deal in town.

No obligation, no tracking, no data, no cookies, not even a breath mint.

Read-a-Latte.

If you decide you like it and want to see how it ends (read the whole book), you can buy the e-book (Kindle) online for the price of a cup of coffee. The coffee is gone in minutes, but the book is yours forever. I've been an Amazon affiliate in good standing for over twenty years, so you're in good hands.

It's the Bookstore Metaphor.

Think of it this way. In most bookstores, you can sit and read free as long as you want. You just can't take the book along when you leave, without first paying for it. Most samples offered online (including Amazon) reveal only the first several pages. My decades of experience leave me feeling totally at ease with having thousands of readers at Galley City 24/7.

Most of my longer works are available in both e-book and print editions. You can also order from Barnes & Noble and most other brick & mortar stores.

Happy Reading!

Read more about my work at Caffeine Books:

www.caffeinebooks.com

About Clocktower Books

Our excellent authors past and present include SF author (Pushcart Prize nominee) A. L. Sirois; Renee Horowitz (*Pharmacy Sleuth Trilogy*); Robin Marchesi (*A Small Journal of Heroin Addiction*, a poetic autobiography in a post-Beat tradition); Deborah Cannon (*Raven Trilogy*); and others including teenage novelist/poet yours truly (*moi*). To learn about our latest offerings, please visit the website at

www.clocktowerbooks.com

Clocktower Books, a pioneering Internet, e-book, and San Diego small press publisher, launched in April 1996 by publishing the world's first entire (not partial) proprietary (not public domain) novels (long works, industry standard) for reading online in HTML format (not for reading on portable media like CD-ROM, floppies, or other intermediary media). Some reviewers are confused and think Gutenberg did this first, but Gutenberg specialize in public domain. We were the first (John Argo: *Neon Blue*, *This Shoal of Space*, *Pioneers*; John T. Cullen: *CON2: The Generals of October)* to publish proprietary novels before e-commerce, during the genesis of e-book and online publishing.

Clocktower Books Museum Site

You will find at the Museum Pages (ever a work in progress) on our webplex a detailed history of our pioneering publishing ventures starting 1996.

www.museum.fyi

From 1998 to 2007, Clocktower Books also published what was, during its decade-long run, the world's first professional Web-only (online) magazine of speculative and dark fiction (or SFFH). See our entry in the SF Encyclopedia under Far Sector SFFH. Visit our Museum for full info.

We published new authors as well as officers and top names of the Science Fiction Writers of America (SFWA); more on our pioneering work at the Science Fiction Encyclopedia online (look under Far Sector).

Our magazine's major names over the years included Deep Outside SFFH and Far Sector SFFH. We published many nominees or later awardees of the Hugo, Nebula, Sturgeon, and other global awards including British, Canadian, and Australian. The leading SF magazine historian Mike Ashley (Liverpool University Press) has stated he will recognize our pioneering magazine in the final volume of his authoritative SF magazine histories.

Selected Titles by John T. Cullen

Suspense & Thrillers writing as John T. Cullen
www.onthrillerstreet.com

Novels and short stories.
Read more about my work at Caffeine Books:
www.caffeinebooks.com

NOVELS INCLUDE:

- Lethal Journey 1892 true crime/famous ghost legend at the Hotel del Coronado near San Diego; my best seller; see **Nonfiction Dead Move** for scholarly analysis on which this novel is closely and accurately based.
- CON2: The Generals of October (a Constitution Thriller;
- Siberian Girl: historical fiction spanning World War Two and the Cold War;
- Orbital Sniper: near-future techno thriller, 21st Century James Gray; his women (not 'girls') mostly have Ph.D., black belts, personalities, and important careers.
- Valley of Seven Castles, a Luxembourg Thriller: a huge thriller, homage to Robert Ludlum (Bourne Identity), and John Buchan (1915 archetype 39 Steps);
- Neon Blue, history's first HTML novel as I call it. Suspense Mystery/Thriller.

Nonfiction Books and Articles

Writing as John T. Cullen

www.readnonfiction.com/

Read more about my work at Caffeine Books:

www.caffeinebooks.com

- Dead Move: The Haunting Mystery of Kate Morgan and the Hotel del Coronado; my scholarly analysis solving the century+ mystery of a tragic crime that drew national attention in 1892. Resulted in a famous ghost legend. From this info, I also wrote a historical novel Lethal Journey.
- Sator Enigma: Ancient Roman Enigma Solved At Last
- Exogravitation: Dark Energy is No More
- Seeking Helen, Finding Homer (release to be announced)
- The God Page: We Are All Animists
- …and more

Journalism and scholarship are in my soul. I hold a B.A. in Liberal Arts from the University of Connecticut (English, Comparative Lit/Classics, Languages); a second B.A. in Computer Information Systems and Accounting (my 'practical degree'), and an M.S. in Business Administration (Boston University). I was a professional writer by age 17 (summer interne reporter, The New Haven Journal-Courier daily CT metro newspaper), a published poet by age 18, and a novelist by age 19 when I completed Summer Planets as a sophomore at UConn. When it comes to nonfiction, I stick with facts and avoid conspiracies etc. Dead Move is deeply researched (by me & hotel's official historian), and Lethal Journey is carefully crafted as a robust thriller closely based on Dead Move.

SF Series Empire of Time

Writing as John Argo
www.empireoftime.com

Read more about my work at Caffeine Books:
www.caffeinebooks.com

NOVELS INCLUDE:

- Summer Planets, my teenage novel completed at 19; a lifetime's work in the Empire of Time series is based on it.
- Mars the Divine
- Orwell in Orbit 2084
- Lantern Road
- Runners: Escape from Prison Planet or Die
- ...and more, spanning a million years and a vast empire of time and space that is only beginning to reveal its powerful secrets with each new story. At least two unconnected short stories, Harps and Night Songs at Um, are integral to the canon.

SF Series DarkSF

Writing as John Argo
www.darksf.com

Read more about my work at Caffeine Books:
www.caffeinebooks.com

NOVELS INCLUDE:

- Doom Spore San Diego
- Meta4City
- YANAPOP (Run for Your Life, a Love Story)
- Streamliners
- Robinson Crusoe 1,000,000 A.D.
- Nebula Express
- This Shoal of Space
- …and more

What is DarkSF?

DarkSF is not gory, splatter, juvenile, or scary. Rather, like the great movies Blade Runner and Inception or the stories of Ray Bradbury, Jorge Luis Borges, or James Tiptree, Jr. (to name a handful of many great examples) DarkSF is artful, rich, atmospheric, beautiful fiction. I like to call it

The Dark Chocolate of SFFH

DarkSF can span multiple genres; most of mine is SF. An exception would be my dark holiday fantasy (Ray Bradbury wrote me a personal rave note) The Christmas Clock.

Short Stories (SFFH, Suspense)

Writing as John Argo and John T. Cullen
www.galleycity.com

Read more about my work at Caffeine Books:
www.caffeinebooks.com

ANTHOLOGIES INCLUDE:

- Night Shots (suspense/mystery/thriller)
- Strange Doors (Weird Tales/DarkSF)
- …and more

Other Works by John T. Cullen*

Including 400+ Poems and Romantic Fiction

www.galleycity.com

Read more about my work at Caffeine Books:

www.caffeinebooks.com

WORKS INCLUDE:

- On Saint Ronan Street, a melancholy, French-style love story written at 27 while stationed as a young U.S. Army soldier in West Germany; set in a New England college town, with strong nods to John Updike; and film The Umbrellas of Cherbourg.
- Cymbalist Poems, one of several poetry anthologies.
- Paris Affaire, a much later (in my 60s) cloned from On Saint Ronan Street, but set in Paris and with a radically different ending.
- …and more

*My birth name (European-U.S.) is Jean Thomas Cullen. As a U.S. Army brat born in Nürnberg, FRG I was named after my two grandfathers—one Luxemburgish, the other U.S.. I find it fun and convenient to hop back & forth among the various pseudonym possibilities this opens up.

www.ingramcontent.com/pod-product-compliance
Lightning Source LLC
LaVergne TN
LVHW091012080826
845145LV00003B/1246

* 9 7 8 0 7 4 3 3 2 3 5 8 1 *